Crossing Lines

Nick Kisella

Nick Kisella

©2014 Nick Kisella

All rights reserved. No part of this book may be reproduced, stored in a retrieval system or transmitted in any form or by any means without the prior written joint permission of the publisher and author, except by a reviewer who may quote brief passages in a review to be printed in a newspaper, magazine or journal.

First Printing

Nick Kisella

DEDICATION

Kim, you and the twins
are my reason to be.
Rich, here's another one-
Thanks for the help Ryan-

Nick Kisella

Nick Kisella

CONTENTS

7	One	30
31	Two	51
52	Three	85
86	Four	102
103	Five	117
118	Six	135
136	Epilogue	139

Nick Kisella

ONE

William Cranston carefully maneuvered his mountain bike around the abandoned cars scattered across the highway. His tired green eyes darted around warily, even though he'd traveled that particular stretch of road so frequently that its configuration had been imbedded in his mind.

"You can never tell if there's someone

new around," he muttered to himself. "Maybe under a car, or jammed between a couple of them, just waiting to get their decrepit hands on me."

Billy, as his family used to call him, didn't like to take chances. At seventeen, he'd already seen his family; parents, die, an older sister, killed, right in front of him, and then he watched his town slowly die off, transforming into hungry walking corpses in a matter of days. He'd survived when the dead rose, and he intended to do everything he could to insure that he continued to survive.

As he steered the bike off the highway he felt himself relax a little, with the threat of the unknown gone. He veered to the right and into the open parking lot of his destination. It was a strip mall. There were only a few abandoned cars and litter strewn about. There were bodies too, but he was so used to seeing them, and smelling them, that they didn't even register in his mind anymore. He immediately spotted a group of six walking corpses staggering into view across the way. Of course, they had to be right by the electronics store he wanted to get into.

"Damn!" His heart suddenly pounded in his chest. "I should be used to this 'Murphy's Law' shit." He sighed, shaking his head, then took a gulp of air and sped up; forcing himself to pedal as fast as his skinny legs could, heading directly for the zombies across the lot.

Billy pulled his right hand off the handlebars and reached back over his shoulder to grasp the aluminum baseball bat that was sticking out of his backpack. It was difficult to do wearing the thick wool coat he had on, but he managed to swing it free just as the first corpse got within striking distance.

"He shoots," Billy shouted as the echo of the bat rang out, smashing the creatures' skull and knocking it to the ground, "He scores!"

Billy spun the bike around, skidding to a halt. He let the backpack slip off his shoulders and fall to the ground while racing toward the remaining dead. They all looked to be in bad shape, and collectively smelled much worse than they looked. One of them barely had any skin on its upper body. He couldn't tell if it was a man or a woman as he took a two-handed swing at it, bashing its head in while quickly spinning around to hit the one behind it. It collapsed to the ground, the echo of its skull cracking open still ringing in Billy's ears seconds later when he turned toward the remaining walking dead.

"Three down, three to go," Billy said, swinging the bat around as if it were a sword. The remaining zombies were shuffling toward him, snarling and hissing. When he turned to look at the closest one, edging up on his left, he did a double-take. "What the fuck-"

It was clearly a female. She still had most

of her hair, which was long and dark. Her face and the hole in the right side of her chest is what struck him as the strangest thing he'd yet seen in his months of destroying the walking corpses.

The woman must have had facial surgery, since one of her cheek implants was hanging half out of her grayish skin. The hole in her chest, where shredded skin still flapped, was from a bite, and it clearly had damaged much more than her skin. Billy stepped back and chuckled. "Holy shit, she got her boob popped!" He couldn't help but laugh at the sight of the empty breast implant swinging separately from the loose skin it had been torn from.

"Sorry lady, but your surgeon did a

terrible job." The bat struck her twice before she fell to the blacktop, with the second blow having enough force behind it to fracture the side of her skull and pop out one of her eyes.

Billy cringed at the gory sight, and took the remaining two down quickly, since they looked to be about his age. He thought he may have recognized one of them, but forced himself not to think about it. He found it difficult enough doing what he was doing, and didn't want to add to it.

Hitting people, living or dead, was something Billy never truly wanted to do. He hated violence. He'd grown up getting picked on for everything from the shape of his body, to his face, to his intelligence, which in spite of anything anyone said, was really rather high. He had ideals though, gained from heroes that he'd read about or watched in cartoons and movies since his early childhood. That, along with everything else, was also why he'd been labeled a 'super-geek' with zits, but since the dead rose, everything had changed. Billy lived in a new world, and he didn't like it very much at all. Life used to at least have rules he could abide by, but in his current situation the only rule that existed was survival.

The initial outbreak, the disease itself, claimed his parents first. It was only after Marshall Law had been declared and their bodies were taken from his house by the military to be disposed of that his sister, Valerie, revealed to him that she too, had become infected.

"I couldn't let them know I was sick. The soldiers, they would have taken me, and I couldn't leave you alone, not yet." Shivering with fever, she held him close, and then pulled away. "I don't have much time, so we have to be quick. You've got to leave, get out of here, find a safe place to hide until this all blows over. Together we can come up with a plan, and you can make it through it all. You've got to!"

He remembered how they cried for what seemed like forever, but it was in fact, only a few minutes before they pulled away from each other and started planning.

There was no time to mourn. No time to feel anything other than urgency and fear.

Billy still hadn't let himself think about what happened long enough to feel anything. He forced himself to go through the motions of his new life as if he were playing a highly advanced game based on virtual reality. It was the only way he'd be able to function.

Stepping away from his latest victims, he knelt down and grabbed his backpack. It was empty except for a bottle of water and a battery powered lantern. He pulled the lantern out and advanced toward the electronics store.

It wasn't a very a large store. The front window had been smashed in and the door was a twisted mess, like most places he'd stolen from. Billy turned the lantern on, and slipped inside between the twisted frame of the door brandishing his bat warily. It was dark inside, but since he knew the layout of the store, he already knew he had to head toward the last aisle in the back, where it was the darkest.

Billy needed a new power converter. The batteries he used were charging well, but his largest DC to AC inverter wasn't working, he needed that if he hoped to use his laptop and the few small appliances he had.

The store was empty a few days earlier when he'd been there, but he knew never to assume a place was truly empty until he'd walked through it first. He wanted to be as quiet as possible, but there was too much glass on the floor. The crackling sound his boots made gave him away to anyone that was inside, living or dead. His grip on the bat tightened, and he felt sweat forming on his forehead, of course, it didn't help that he was wearing a thick wool coat, and ski pants. He always dressed that way when going out, thinking that it was at least marginal protection against being bitten if he was ever caught in a bind. He didn't think the dead would be able to bite through what he wore, and though his strategy had never been put to the test, he felt safer that way.

The thought of being stuck inside the store and suddenly surrounded, terrified Billy, but he pushed on, walking across the front of the aisles. When he was sure there was nothing moving around he walked to the back, stopping in the stockroom first. There was nothing there he hadn't seen before, so he went to the aisle where the inverters were and gabbed one. It was heavier than he expected, but he was still able to carry it under his arm while shining the lantern in front.

When he got outside he noticed that it had gotten very cloudy.

"It better not rain, I didn't put the barrel on the roof today," Billy mumbled with a curse under his breath. After returning the lantern to his backpack and zipping the inverter inside one of the larger sections, he shrugged it back over his shoulders and got on the bike. He could hear the growling of the dead lurking somewhere nearby, but he couldn't see them yet.

That was as good a reason as any to hightail it out of there.

The ride back to Billy's 'Sanctuary', as he liked to think of it, was uneventful until he reached the underpass near the train station.

There was a motorcycle that he hadn't seen before. It must have smashed into one of the abandoned cars, the front fork was bent and the driver was nowhere to be seen. Billy sped up, hoping he could reach whoever was on the bike before the dead that lingered in the area did. He got to the top of the hill above the underpass and pushed himself even harder when he heard gunfire.

The bike spun gravel as Billy turned

left. The train station loomed ahead. It was a foreboding sight, with several cars smashed into it, all the glass shattered, and partially devoured bodies covered in congealed gore strewn about.

    Billy spotted a man in a flannel shirt and jeans trying to fight off a small gathering of the dead. They had him surrounded and were closing in on him. He had a rifle, but there were just too many of them. Billy leaned back and squeezed both handbrakes tightly. The bike jerked to a halt. He let it drop between his legs and slid off the backpack while running toward the man. The baseball bat was still crusted with bits of bone and brain from earlier. He swung it high and hard at the nearest creature, sending it sprawling to the blacktop. He moved on to the next one, and the next, until finally, between the man in flannel and himself, all the dead had been reduced to piles of unmoving decaying flesh and bone.

Billy let the bat fall to the ground and leaned over, hands on his knees, panting, heart thumping in his chest like a jackhammer. After a minute or so he caught his breath and turned toward the man he had fought alongside.

"You okay?" His voice crackled from the dryness of his throat. "My name's Billy. I've got a place setup about a mile up the tracks." He said, gesturing to the railroad tracks.

The man leaned back against the rear

bumper of a car, still breathing heavy himself. He ran a hand through his hair to get it out of his eyes and slowly shook his head.

Billy's heart sank. He rushed over to the man, leaving the bat on the ground, but stopped dead when the man held up his left hand in a halting gesture.

"It's only a little one," the man said, sounding defeated, "but that's all it takes."

"Oh my god," Billy said, taking a step forward. He could see the bite stretching from the side of his wrist to the palm of his hand. The blood, dark and thick, was dripping from his fingertips.

"Maybe we can stop the infection somehow." Billy said trying to sound hopeful, his mind trying to grasp at anything he learned about first aid since the outbreak.

"It's not like I can cut my hand off," the man said, angrily. He closed his injured hand into a fist, grunting with the pain of the effort. "I already lost the person I was traveling with. Looks like I'll never make it to the cabin after all." His words were quiet, a whisper of confirmation more to himself than to Billy.

"I'm sorry." Head downcast, Billy was at a loss for words. The man was the first survivor he'd seen in weeks. He had hope for a moment there during the heat of fighting the dead; he should have known better.

"Is there anything I can do for you, anyway I can help you?" Billy asked, barely above a whisper. "I'm so sorry I didn't get here sooner."

"It's not your fault." The man said, crouching to sit on the ground. "There is something you can do for me though."

"Yeah?" Billy looked at him hopefully.

"Yeah, I'm out of ammo. I need you to finish me off before I turn into one of those things." The man said looking up at him.

Billy's eyes widened with shock and a chill of fear.

"But, you're still alive." He said to the man. "I don't even know your name. I don't have a gun or anything like that either. I can't kill you. I've never killed anyone before, not anyone alive."

"I'm Joe, just Joe." He grimaced, a jolt of pain shot up his arm and he suddenly felt nauseous. "This bite makes me dead already. You seem pretty good with that bat of yours. Just give me a good one to the head. Give it all ya got."

Billy was trembling. He felt a horrible mixture of emotions churning around inside him and he was so confused a dull ache began to throb in the back of head.

"I, I can't do it, I just can't." He stuttered. "I can't kill somebody that's still alive."

"Please." Joe whispered, eyes pleading. "You can't leave me like this. I don't want to turn into one of those things."

It felt as if time had frozen, and Billy stood there in silence, with only his fear thrashing around in his belly. He remembered the same feeling when his sister was shot down helping him escape their house. The soldiers saw her sweating, how red her eyes were, and they shot her down without a word.

Billy ran as fast as he could, and barely made it out of his neighborhood alive.

His vision cleared suddenly, and his face had no expression. The numbness he'd experienced before had returned as if with the flick of a switch. He silently turned away from Joe and went over to get the bat.

The bat felt cold in his hands, but the weight of it felt right, as if he belonged carrying it. His movements were mechanical as he stepped over to where Joe sat with his head down. The man nodded, he knew what was coming, and stared straight ahead, as if he were looking through Billy and not actually at him.

Absently, Billy sucked in a deep breath, quickly swinging the bat over his head with both hands. Staring at Joe blankly, he swung down with all the strength he could muster.

The sound didn't register to Billy, but he knew full well that he'd smashed Joe's skull, killing him immediately. That didn't stop the rage from suddenly exploding out of him, rage for everything and how it all became nothing. Billy swung the bat again and again, each blow weaker than the last as the rage ebbed. For those few minutes he felt as if he had left his body and watched himself swinging the bat.

Billy felt as if the life had been drained out of him. He turned away trembling, confused and woozy. Joe's body, head battered to a pulp, still twitched as Billy slid the backpack over his shoulders and got back on his bike. He didn't want to leave the body there as it was, but there was nothing he could do. He didn't even have anything to cover it with.

"I guess he's just another body among all the bodies, dead or undead." He mumbled.

His legs felt like lead making the short trip back to his self proclaimed sanctuary.

In his heart he knew nothing would ever be the same again. His heart told him it was the right thing to do, but his mind told him it was still murder.

"So much for sticking to that ideal." He thought.

TWO

Billy reached the freight train sooner than he expected, but since the incident at the train station time felt as if it had swirled into slow motion. It had gotten much cloudier but it was still light outside. He had been riding on the street that ran parallel to the train tracks, which had been constructed higher up on a hill.

As Billy rode into the shadow of the train he slowed to a stop. He got off the bike still feeling numb inside. Moving mechanically, with his legs sore and tired, he pulled the bike up the hill to the train. The baseball bat felt good in his hand as he scanned the area before continuing on up the tracks.

"The last thing I need right now is more of those dead things." He said gruffly. "I'm so fuckin' tired I'm liable to trip on my own feet and end up somebody's dinner."

A dozen cars up from the caboose Billy found his hidden sanctuary. He sighed loudly, beyond relieved.

In front of him, connected between a tanker car and an empty flat car stretched a forty foot long freight car. It was gunmetal gray and about nine feet high. Billy saw the old freight car as home, his own creation and safe haven.

Months earlier, after weeks of trying to hide out in abandoned houses and stores, always on the run from either the military or the dead, he set out to leave town carrying only a crowbar. Some soldiers spotted him and he had to run for it.

Racing through yards, narrowly eluding the military and the hordes of dead that roamed his neighborhood streets, Billy had stumbled upon the train. He was trying to avoid the main roads at the time when he found the empty train tracks that ran through town. He was following them and then out of the blue it was there, right in front of him like an enormous monument to a forgotten age.

When he first saw the train he wondered what happened, and why it had been stopped where it was, especially with the train station so close. Then he checked the front car and knew why after he saw what was left of the driver.

The uniform the man wore was torn up and covered in congealed gore. His face had been literally torn off, eyes and all, leaving only the shredded muscle beneath and that had begun to rot. Billy's stomach lurched, but he bit it back, forcing himself not to breathe in the foul stench, not to puke; even when he saw the stump of the man's right arm, the bones picked clean a few feet away.

"At least he stopped the train before it could derail and crash into anything." Billy said, trying to put the sight of the dead man out of his mind as he slid the door to the engine compartment shut. He wondered if there were any lingering zombies in the area, and searched around the train nervously. To his surprise, other than another dead uniformed man on the tracks, he was alone. He searched the train cars to see if there was anything he could use inside them or if there was a safe place for him to stay the night.

When he reached the freight train he knew he'd hit the jackpot.

Being on his own for as long he'd been, there was nothing to do except survive and think. After finding the empty freight car and claiming it as his own, he'd found safety. The dead would have no way to get into his steel fortress. That's when all the 'thinking' took place and he was able to turn the vast dark emptiness into a safe haven and breathe a little easier.

"If I'm stuck here for the duration, the least I can do is get some of the comforts of home." He declared, already envisioning how he could set things up inside.

For lights and other things he decided to use solar power, knowing enough about it from science class and his own curiosity for 'Green Energy'. He thought the flat roof of the car was perfect for it. With no trees or buildings to block it, the sun would always shine on it. From there it was simple.

It had taken many trips and well over a week to set things up to his satisfaction, but since he was alone, it wasn't very difficult to get in and out of places quickly to take what he needed. He'd gotten used to slipping in and out of places quietly, and if he had to bash in a few of the dead along the way he did without thinking about it.

The military presence in the area had lessened, and he'd taken a mountain bike from someone's garage to get around with. The most difficult thing for him to do was get larger items on his bike and then up into the freight car itself. The solar panels were fragile but sturdy enough to travel with once he learned how to tie two of them together and carry them strapped to his back.

Looking at it from the outside, there was nothing unusual about the freight car. There were two wide doors on each side of it, but they were sealed shut. Billy had even locked them from the inside to make sure there was no way to open them. There was no other way inside the car, except for the opening that Billy had made through a vent in the roof. To get there, he had to climb a ladder on the backend of the freight car.

Zombies didn't know how or simply couldn't climb ladders, but Billy had more to worry about than merely the walking dead trying to get inside. There were scavengers too, and unlike regular survivors like him, he'd seen them kill for a pair of shoes or the smallest morsel of food. So he had to beef things up a bit concerning security.

Perched on the roof, next to the ladder, was a tiny webcam. It was wireless, and the feed went directly to a small laptop he had inside the car. If anyone made an attempt to climb the ladder, he'd not only hear it, he'd be able to see it, as long as his batteries had power. He'd placed a few others around the roof of the freight car as well, just so he could look around while inside.

Billy also fashioned an escape hatch if he ever needed to get out quick. It was on the other side of the car, cut into the old timbers that made up that section of the floor. He made a thick panel to cover the opening and bolted a deadbolt on each side to hold it in securely.

As for weapons, Billy didn't know the slightest thing about guns and with no one around to show him, he decided not to take any he found or attempt using one. He never liked guns anyway, and really didn't want one.

"I'd probably just end up shooting myself in the foot anyway." He thought to himself. "The idea of running out of ammo at the wrong time doesn't exactly thrill me either."

Instead of guns, he'd gotten together a collection of aluminum baseball bats, a few machetes, some hunting knives and a hatchet.

The mountain bike made getting

around easy. It was quiet and he found that he could get around a crowd of the living dead easily. It kept him in shape too.

When Billy reached the back of the freight car, near the ladder, he untied a thin cord of nylon rope he had coiled around the mountain bike under the seat. It was long enough to hold in his hand while he climbed up the ladder, and when he reached the top, he was able to pull up the lightweight bike and lay it flat in the middle of the roof, making it difficult to see from the street. He looked across the rest of the long roof, and stood up carefully, still not comfortable with heights.

A quick visual of the solar panels spaced out across the sides of the roof showed him all was well. Nothing had been damaged by wind or covered in debris. He considered his method of gathering power his 'masterpiece' and the only thing that kept him sane. With the solar panels constantly collecting energy to charge the vast array of batteries he had below, there was never a worry about being in the dark; or in his case, without a hot meal, music or movies.

"I couldn't live without my music or movies." He said after taking a couple of IPods and portable DVD players from a store weeks ago. He took a case full of movies and CD's as well to keep himself occupied.

At the far end of the roof he'd set up his entrance. All the cables from the solar panels were taped together and led there.

Originally there was a vent in the roof. Billy had taken the cover off and replaced it with a thick piece of wood he'd gotten from a building supply a short distance away. He'd cut a small notch in it so the snake of wires would fit through, connected hinges and a padlock to it just in case anyone found his home while he was gone. It wasn't the sturdiest but it would give anyone without a key at least a little trouble if they tried to get in. The lock was still there untouched, so he unlocked it and flipped the door open.

Another ladder descended from the opening in the roof. Billy lowered himself down into the darkness, flipped the door shut again and reached around blindly until he felt the lamp he'd hung from the ceiling.

With the flick of a switch he had light. It was a small camping lantern but it illuminated the area just enough for him to see where he was going.

The interior of the freight car was laid out like a narrow apartment. He had a small kitchen area where he kept his food and water in boxes and sacks. There was a short table with a camping stove on it next to a metal folding chair. Of late, he'd acquired a blue plastic barrel that he used to collect rain water. It was never too much, but it came in handy when he was running low on bottled water.

Further down he had an inflatable couch that he'd taken from a camping store. There was a folding table and chair next to it.

That was also where he kept his laptop and where the wires from the solar panels connected to his charge controller, batteries and converter. He had several battery chargers already hooked up, and there were a couple of flashlights there charging too. He took one, clicked it on, and shined it on his handy work. It looked like a piled up mess, but it suited his needs and he wasn't concerned about how it looked as long as it worked.

Billy immediately took off his pack and set about connecting his new converter. He pulled the old one off and tossed it to the side, then hooked up the new one. When he was sure everything was connected properly he turned away from it and walked further down into the freight car to where he had an air mattress. There was a pile of clothes next to it. They were new and clean, some still in their packaging. Clothes were mostly disposable. When he ran low he just took more from anywhere he could and got rid of the old stuff.

Billy turned on a lamp next to the mattress, put down his flashlight and stripped out of his ski pants and heavy coat. He debated going to the bathroom, which consisted of a portable RV toilet at the back wall of the car where he also had extra batteries stacked, but decided against it, too tired to take the walk.

Flopping down on the mattress, he finally felt safe. He grabbed an IPod that was lying on the mattress next to his pillow and put a single ear bud in one of his ears before turning on some classical music.

Classical music relaxed him.

Leaning back, he felt the wall that he formed inside himself earlier in the day come crumbling down as the gentle sounds of Vivaldi filled his head.

"I killed a man today." He said hoarsely. His words echoed around him, a hollow sound in the dim light. He squeezed his eyes shut and wanted to scream, but instead turned over, away from the light, and cried like he hadn't allowed himself to since it all began.

*****

Billy didn't know how long he slept, but

when he woke up his arms and legs were sore and he had a headache. He checked the small clock he kept on what served as the kitchen table and saw that it was nearly noon.

"Damn, half the day is gone." He shook his head, disappointed. "I guess it doesn't matter, it's not like I really had any urgent plans other than scavenging a bit anyway."

Before the dead came back to life and Billy still lived at home with his family, they always ate their meals with the television on. He'd tried to regain a sense of normalcy while in the freight car, his new home, so he always ate with a movie playing since there was no television. That afternoon he was downing a couple of Pop Tarts while reclined on the couch, watching the end of a low-budget horror movie he used to like. It was actually filmed a few towns over and he'd met the guys that made it once.

"I wonder if they're still alive?" He mumbled absently. "I guess it doesn't matter, their movie making days are over, regardless." He chuckled dryly. "Just like everything else."

He tried not to think about it. Usually avoiding it like that worked, but ever since he'd finished setting up the freight car, when he actually had time on his hands and wasn't fearfully in constant danger, anger and depression threatened him like a bully on a street corner, and he knew more than his fair share of them.

Billy honestly didn't mind being alone all

that much. He was used to it, and thought it was cool that he could have pretty much anything he wanted. The idea that it had to be that way because there was no one else alive is what bothered him. The idea that everywhere he went there were either unmoving dead bodies or moving dead bodies that wanted to take a chunk out of him, now that was downright depressing.

He finally got up and went to the back of the freight car to use the toilet and wash up. He had a basin back there with soap and a bucket of water for washing. It wasn't the greatest, but he was happy to be able to clean up and not smell as bad as the walking dead anymore.

Some fresh clothes made him feel a little

better. He pulled on his ski pants and after looking through his pile of weapons, clipped the hatchet to his belt. Then he grabbed his wool coat and checked the cameras around the freight car to see if it was safe to go out.

"No visitors today," he joked after scanning through the video feeds. "It's time to head out and see what I can see and get what I can get."

THREE

Tony Marelli sped around the back of 'The Taj', narrowly avoiding a horde of zombies, cursing angrily under his breath. He couldn't believe what he was seeing. The zombies had broken through the front gate and had somehow gotten into the house.

The house itself was a broken mess. All the windows on the ground floor were shattered and the doors were pushed in. He noticed even the lower basement door had been broken in as he swung the SUV around. The only reassuring thing he noticed right off was Joe's Jeep; it was gone.

"I hope he got away safe with Sam," he thought to himself, thinking a silent prayer for them both.

"This place is huge." His son Tom said from the back seat.

"That's why we used to call it 'The Taj'." Tony's eyes widened as he clipped a zombie with the front bumper. "The owner was a real whack-job with more money and time on her hands then she knew what to do with."

"I thought you said it was supposed to be like a fortress." Tom said, squinting, his face practically pressed to the window.

"It was!" Tony shouted nervously, "But look how many of those things there are walking around! We'll be lucky if we can get out of here in one piece!"

The SUV was thumping over bodies and body parts that were already on the ground when they got there, while Tony swung the wheel left and right as if he were playing some crazy console game trying to avoid the worst of it. If he could have kicked himself he would have. He knew trying to get back to Joe and Samantha at 'The Taj' wasn't a great idea, but he'd had hope. It would have been a great place to stop on the way to the cabin to rest and get some supplies. Seeing Joe and Samantha would have been great too, but unfortunately too much time had passed, and the dead had virtually taken over everything.

"Is there any place safe to stop?" His wife Amy asked. She was sitting next to him and gone pale since seeing the gory mob around the enormous house. "We've been on the run since yesterday. We've all got to get some rest."

"Let me get us out of here first!" Tony said gunning the engine again. He tried to avoid hitting anyone because he was afraid he'd smash the grill and radiator, and overheating would strand them among an army of dead; a sure death sentence.

The zombies were following the SUV. Most of them were slow moving but it didn't matter if he couldn't get out of the infested neighborhood and onto an open road.

He frantically spun the wheel and crossed the street, bursting through a short picket fence and continuing on through the backyard of a neighboring house. The truck crashed through patio chairs and knocked over a gas grill before turning and hitting the street again, which luckily, was clear.

He still had the slip of paper that Samantha had giving him with directions to a cabin that was supposed to be safe and filled with supplies. He pulled that paper out of his pocket, took note of what was written on it and spun the truck around, heading there.

"We should have just gone to the cabin in the first place!" He said angrily, thinking back to when he was last at 'The Taj'. "I should never have risked everything to get here."

"Tony, it's okay," Amy said quietly. "You didn't know how bad things would be."

Tony nodded, still irritated with himself.

When Tony left 'The Taj' after the outbreak began, he raced home like a bat out of hell. Things were already getting bad. The streets were filled with cars and dead people were everywhere. He was so worried about his wife being alone in the house and the kids being away at college that he drove like a madman, letting nothing bar his path. He thought he had to pick up his wife and then somehow track down his kids at school.

When he finally got home, after white-knuckle driving six hours on a trip that would normally only take one, he found his wife, son, Tom and daughter, Sophie, locked in the basement. His wife Amy had his shotgun and nearly blew his head off when he opened the door. Tony was more than relieved to see them all together and safe, but nearly soiled his pants when he had the barrel of the shotgun shoved in his face so abruptly.

Amy told him that the kids were already on their way home when the outbreak hit the news and all the insanity started.

"They were worried about us," she said, once he was inside and a little calmer, "so they came home sooner than they were originally planning to."

"Thanks for holding it together, and

keeping everyone safe. I'll get my .38 and meet you in the basement," Tony said, hugging his wife tightly. "I'm so glad you're all home safe."

And that was the way it was for over a month. Tony and his family locked down the house as best as they could. They covered the windows with plywood, barred the doors, and stayed in the basement. It was a finished basement, with a bathroom and a bar. They took all the food they had downstairs with them and hoped they could wait things out.

They had a television, and though there were only a few emergency announcements being made each day, the military was said to have things under control.

They were wrong.

The broadcasts soon stopped.

Within a week most of the military went AWOL after realizing what they were up against. So many soldiers fell to the dead just because they failed to listen to their superiors and aim for the head, thinking they were killing innocent civilians. Their ranks became a confused jumble of people getting killed by their own without even realizing why until it was too late.

Eventually Marshall Law was declared and normal innocent people were getting shot down trying to escape to safety while the walking dead trudged on, killing more people and gaining numbers. Eventually there were no safe places to escape to. Many of the shelters set up by the government were overrun by the dead enemy with nowhere left to go.

Tony and his family waited it out in the basement as best as they could. They only occasionally ventured upstairs to quietly check on things and peek outside. After a week the power went out, but Tony had a propane generator that kicked on automatically. Because of that, and using anything powered with electricity very sparingly, they had a few extra days of power and running water.

That didn't stop the dead from breaking into the house. The crashing sound, so loud and powerful that Tony thought the entire house shuddered, happened early in the morning. It came out of nowhere and everyone woke up terrified, but he was there to calm them down and keep them quiet.

They could hear the dead above them, shuffling around, smashing into things. Glass shattered, things crashed to the floor. The moaning and hissing sounds the dead made were what got to them the most, especially Amy, who thought of the house as an extension of herself.

"Those things are up there!" She held back her tears, but Tony could see she was about to lose it. "They could break in down here any minute!"

"That's not going to happen Amy," he said holding her close. "We've got a steel skinned door that's totally secure at the top of the stairs, and another leading to the garage.

If we're quiet enough, they won't even know we're here."

"But, they're destroying everything we own!" She was shaking when she spoke to Tony. "Everything we've built is gone."

Tony pulled her aside, behind the bar where the kids couldn't hear them at all.

"Honey, everything we've built is right here," he gestured to where the kids were trying to stay calm by playing scrabble. "Everything upstairs can be replaced. We'll get through this, one way or another. Please, trust me, we'll be okay if we just stick together and stay quiet. We couldn't get out safely now anyway, there's too many of them here."

So they stayed there, but from then on

they spoke in hushed tones, tried to be as quiet as possible, and never even made an attempt to go upstairs again.

Eventually the noise upstairs stopped. They could still hear a few of them roaming around in the house, but the majority of them left after not finding a meal there.

By the time a month passed, they were running out of supplies. They were even running out of candles. Tony knew they had to do something or they'd be plunged into darkness soon, and there wouldn't be any coming back from that.

He came up with a plan, a way to get out and get to 'The Taj', where they could either stay with Joe and Samantha, or move on to the cabin Sam talked about. He still had the directions she'd given him the day he left after he put Richie out of his misery. Either way, it was better than what they were currently doing, which would only end in disaster.

"You're fucking crazy for even suggesting that!" Amy whispered angrily. "How can you even-"

"Amy, honey calm down," Tony said, grasping her hands with a slight gesture toward the kids, who were standing right by them so they could hear too. When he saw that she'd regained control of herself he went on with his plan.

"Anyway, as I was saying. We don't know if they've broken into the garage or not." Tony spoke completely calm, even though he wanted to shout his words and curse the dead that had taken over his house and changed his life and the lives of his family forever. "We've got the two guns, and I'm sure we have a bat or two still down here somewhere from when Sophia played softball, maybe even a hockey stick or two from Tommy's hockey days. Now I've dealt with these things before. They don't move that well, so even if they have gotten into the garage, we can probably take enough of them down and get to your SUV." He looked directly at his wife and Amy nodded, shaking, but calm. "You've got the garage door opener in your truck, so all you have to do is press the button and floor it. We need to avoid using the guns unless we absolutely have to because the noise will only draw more to us. Now I suggest we pack up anything we can use in the backpacks we have. If there's more, we can try to carry it in a trash bag."

"Daddy, what if there's too many of them?" Sophia asked fearfully. "How are we supposed to get out of here? I saw the news before we got here. One bite and you're dead, you become infected and then one of them."

Sophia was a very strong girl, and Tony had never seen her afraid of anything, not even a bully twice her size when she was ten, but she was standing there close to tears.

"We'll be okay, honey." He assured her, gripping her shoulder firmly. "Trust me.

Like I said, I've dealt with a few of these things already, they look much worse than they actually are. The big problem isn't them it's how many of them there are. The garage isn't that big, so not many could fit in there even if they have broken in. We can do this. Just think that in your head, 'We can do this'. Now let's get going."

They had everything packed up. Tony, carrying one of Sophia's old softball bats, was leading them out. He'd given his .38 to Tommy, who was only supposed to use it if he had to, and even then, head shots, always head shots. Amy and Sophia were following them, with Amy holding the shotgun, and the keys to the SUV. The truck, with all of its bells and whistles, was still her pride and joy.

Tony slowly unbolted and unlocked the basement door leading out to the garage as quietly as he could; opening it slowly, Tom directly behind him pointed the pistol at the opening. He stepped out as quietly as he could and looked around. When he saw that there was no one there, he turned back to the rest of them and nodded with a determined grin, continuing on.

It wasn't until he'd stepped away from the door that he saw the first of the dead lurking around the inside of his garage. He was directly behind the door Tony had just opened. It was his sixty-year-old neighbor, unfortunately also the one neighbor he liked and got along well with. The stench he was giving off made Tony swallow back bile. The man's throat had been torn open, with bits of rotting flesh still hanging around his exposed windpipe. Tony's eyes widened, and as terror gripped him so did anger. He swung the bat as hard as he could at the man's head.

"You miserable fuck, you're not gettin' me or my family!" he whispered angrily under his breath.

Tom got into the garage just as his father had swung the bat. He saw it collide with their neighbor, Dan Wilson's head, caving in his skull, and though his stomach quaked at the sight of Dan, he quickly raised the .38 up high, aiming for anyone else he could see.

Stepping further into the garage, he

ushered out both his mother and sister, leading them away, around the back of the SUV while making sure that no one was behind them.

Tony had stayed by the door, standing over Dan's body. He scanned the rest of the garage and saw that the side door had been broken into. It was wide open, and several zombies were walking in from that door. Tom aimed his gun, but before he could fire it Tony ran to him and pulled his arm down.

"No! The noise will bring more!" He whispered urgently. "Just get the girls into the truck, I'll cover you!"

Tony raced around the front of the SUV to head off the zombies coming inside while Tom brought his mother and sister around to the driver's side of the truck. Amy got in and with trembling hands slipped the key into the ignition. She waited for everyone else to get in before she started the engine and hit the switch to raise the garage door.

"C'mon Tony, damn it!" she said to herself. "Hurry up!"

Tony smacked Dan's wife, Margaret, who was missing most of an arm and covered in blood, hard in the side of the head. Her skull split like a ripe melon and she fell to the floor, a bloody unmoving heap. Heart racing, he saw that the there were only two others coming for him, but they were behind her. They looked like two teenagers. One of them had an enormous belly wound, with his intestines torn up and hanging over his slow moving legs. The other was missing part of his face. They were growling and hissing, moving awkwardly, shuffling as if their ankles were tied together, and since Margaret was on the ground he knew they would have to struggle to get around her. Tony saw that as his way out, so he made a dash back to the SUV, jumping in on the passenger side.

"Go!" He shouted to his wife when he slammed the door shut.

Amy flipped the key, started the SUV and opened the garage door at the same time.

She revved the engine as the door slowly rose up. The two remaining zombies in the garage had just about reached the truck, with more coming in behind them, when Amy slammed the shifter into drive. The SUV sped forward, barely clearing the bottom edge of the door and narrowly avoiding the zombies. They shot down the driveway and into a crowd of the dead blocking the road.

"Oh shit!" she yelled, trying to turn away from them. Tony grabbed the wheel and spun it to the left, away from the majority of the creatures. They took down their neighbors' mailbox and the back of the truck spun into a few of them, hitting hard enough to rock the vehicle, but they'd gotten away from the crowd.

"We can't run through that many of them head-on," he said, letting go of the wheel with a sigh. "They'll smash the front end and then we'll be stuck in the middle of the mob!"

"Tony, I think you'd better drive, at least for now." Amy said nervously. "I'm liable to get us killed. I need some time to calm down."

They drove the entire day and on into the night, avoiding major roads, and anywhere else they saw zombies. By morning, they'd reached 'The Taj', but were running low on fuel and exhausted.

"We need to find somewhere to stop and rest a bit." Amy said. She was much calmer, trying to get used to what she was seeing and what they were doing.

"We need gas too." Tony looked at

the gauge and shook his head. "It's a good thing you always keep your tank full. We would have been screwed if you didn't."

Tony kept driving, but slower, avoiding the gas pedal as much as he could. They were driving into a town. The streets we more empty than they'd seen thus far, Tony thought it might have been because most people either tried to stay in their homes or got stuck on the highways trying to escape somewhere.

"Maybe we can find a place to stop around here?" Sophia said, looking around. "It doesn't look like there are that many of those things walking around."

"We're going to have to either way," Tony sighed. "We're riding on fumes."

"There's a strip mall ahead," Tom pointed between his parents from the back seat, "with a gas station on the corner. Maybe we can fuel up there and get some supplies."

"The pumps aren't going to be working, but we might be able to siphon some from the cars in the lot if I can get a length of hose." Tony said, heading in that direction. "We can definitely use some food and water too. I hope the stores haven't been completely picked clean."

"There's got to be something left." Amy said, "We're just going to need a flashlight. I think I have one in the back of the truck."

Tony could see a few zombies off in the

distance, a couple of blocks away. It would take a while at the speed they walked to reach them, and even if they did, it wouldn't take much to finish them off.

"Everybody look around. If you see any of those things walking around say something quick." He pulled into the gas station parking lot slipping the SUV between two parked cars at the side of the building. "The only ones I can see are down the road over there." He said pointing to them.

They all looked around, but saw nothing. It was like a ghost town, eerily quiet.

"I think we'd better get moving." Tony said, taking off his seatbelt. "The sooner we get what we need and get out of here the better. Maybe if we're lucky we can find a house or something to hold up in for the night."

"That would be great." Sophie sighed. "A few hours of real sleep would feel so good right now."

"I wouldn't care if we had to park in someone's garage and just sleep in the truck." Tom said.

"Yeah, as long as we could get the door shut and lock ourselves in." Tony said.

"Let's get started. I think we should split up." Amy looked at Tony, waiting for him to argue against it. "It'll take less time."

"Normally, I'd say you're crazy, but you're right, it's probably a smart thing to do under the circumstances even though I'm paranoid." Tony agreed. She had a logical point and he wasn't about to argue about it, especially as tired as he was. He simply quirked his brow up at her and grinned. "We have weapons, and we'll be pretty close to each other even split into two groups. Sophia, you stay with me." Tony looked at his daughter. "There's an air compressor on the side of the building. You can keep an eye on things while I cut a piece of the hose off and start siphoning gas."

"Tommy and I will hit that little convenience store in the strip mall across the street." Amy said to him.

"Tom, Mom, just 'Tom'," Tom smirked at her. "I'm a little old for 'Tommy' these days."

"Sure Thomas." She said with a wink. "Hey, I'm your mother and I'm exhausted, deal with it."

"Now remember Tom," Tony said. "Don't use the .38 unless you absolutely have to, and-"

"I know, 'headshots, only headshots'." He chuckled dismissively. "Am I suddenly twelve again?"

Amy got her flashlight from the back of the car along with a trash bag she emptied of clothes for anything they might find. She also took one of the two softball bats they brought with them, handing the shotgun to her husband.

"We should each have a gun." She said before leaving with Tom.

"You still know how to use this thing?" Tony asked his daughter as he handed her the shotgun.

"I'm still at the firing range once a month even without you there." Sophie said.

"I hope you're as good a shot as ever." He pulled out a sharp pocketknife and went over to cut the hose. His eyes darted around but thankfully saw nothing unusual.

There was a five-gallon bucket at the gas pumps full of murky water. Tony grabbed it and spilled out the water. He took a long black funnel that was sitting by the oil display next to the kiosk.

Looking over the cars parked there, he decided to try the Cadillac first, thinking that it had to have a large gas tank. It may very have, but he was only able to fill the bucket up halfway.

Tony cursed under his breath. He brought the bucket over to the SUV and using the funnel, dumped it in the gas tank.

"It's not much of a start, but if something crazy happens and we have to get out here fast at least we won't be riding on fumes anymore." He said to Sophie.

"Yeah, but I'm keeping my fingers crossed that nothing happens." She nodded. "I still can't believe this is going on. It's completely insane! What could have possibly caused it?"

"I have no idea. They never really said what caused it on TV either, though they didn't overrule terrorism." Tony said shaking his head. "We don't even have any way to find out if the rest of the world is going through what we're going through, or if it's just us. If it's truly a virus and airborne I would guess it's all over."

He started to siphon a Toyota close enough to keep talking with Sophie. "The toughest part of doing this is trying to make sure you don't swallow any gas." Tony spit out the small amount of gas that he got in his mouth while twisting the hose down and into the bucket. It started to fill, the scent of the fuel and the bitter taste of it making him nauseous.

"Dad, those two dead people are getting awfully close to us." Sophie lifted the rifle and got them in her sites. "Should I take them down now or wait for them to get closer?"

"Why don't you wait a bit, but I think it might be easier for me to bash their heads in anyway. It'll save ammo and be quieter too." Tony said, still feeling woozy. "We don't know how many of those things are around. The last thing we want to do is attract a mob of them by making too much noise." He looked around nervously.

FOUR

The store was a disgusting mess.

The door had been ripped off its hinges, and the front window was long gone. Tom walked in reluctantly. His first impulse was to gag at the smell of sour milk and mold. He fought back the nausea while trying to avoid stepping on the bits of glass all over the floor, his mother, right on his heels. He doubted they would find anything useful inside, but he continued on is spite of that just to make sure.

Amy shined the flashlight across the front section of aisles, its glare reflecting back to her from what remained of a security mirror at the back of the store. She saw no movement, heard nothing, so she gently nudged Tom to move and they both traveled further inside, the darkness gradually engulfing them in its cold murk.

The floor was covered in empty wrappers and bits of rotten food. There were torn open cartons of cigarettes strewn about like confetti. Most of the shelves were either empty or full of trash. Amy saw what she thought was a boot on the floor at the end of an aisle and stopped dead. She pointed to it and Tom turned, heading off in that direction, gripping the pistol in both hands with her close behind.

Suddenly there was a scraping sound. Tom stepped back apprehensively, grabbing his mothers' arm to steer the flashlight to where he thought the noise was coming from, but there was nothing there.

Tom thought it may have been a rat or some other rodent they probably disturbed by coming in, but then the boot he was looking at moved, and he heard the strange scraping sound again. Tom rushed forward and saw it lying there, struggling to move.

It was a dead man. He was covered in gore, lying on his stomach, missing an arm and most of a leg. The dead man was dragging himself forward with his remaining boney, sore encrusted gray hand.

Amy stepped ahead of Tom, totally grossed out by the sight of the zombie's black nails scraping across the tiles but poised to bash the thing in the head when they both heard something crash on the other side of the store. Then glass shattered at the rear of the store and the moaning began.

"There must be more of them in the freezers!" Tom shouted panic stricken, abruptly breaking the silence. "Let's get the hell out of here."

They headed for the front entrance, but saw that somehow a few of the dead had silently crept up on them, barring their way out.

"The window!" Amy yelled, pulling her son's arm.

They ran around the counter and were about to climb outside when Amy felt something grip her around the ankle so tightly she gasped with pain. She looked down and saw the upper half of a woman on the floor under the window. Amy cringed when she saw the exposed spinal cord wiggle and twist among rotting entrails as the creature dragged herself closer. She'd grabbed Amy's ankle and was trying to pull herself forward, snapping her jaws at the open air, trying to bite her leg. Amy could feel the creature's hot breath on her as she tried to no avail to kick herself free.

"Mom look out!" Tom shouted,

jumping in front of her. He quickly shot the zombie in the head. The shot echoed loudly in the dismal store, and bits of dark liquid gore rained over the area behind the counter.

Still the hand clung to Amy's ankle.

Tom stepped on the arm and pulled his mother's leg free, then put his arm around her and helped her through the window. He followed her over just as the slow moving zombies reached the opening themselves, hissing and grunting.

They hit the street, both of them running toward the gas station as a stream of the dead came around the side of the building, clawing at the air, hungrily following them. Amy nearly fell over after a few strides, her ankle sending jolts of hot pain up her leg. She caught herself and didn't fall, but couldn't do more than hobble on toward the garage.

Tom didn't know he'd left his mother behind.

"Dad!" Tom shouted, "Get the truck started! We gotta get out of here!" He saw his father drop the bucket he was carrying and watched Sophie aim the shotgun in his direction.

"Are you okay?" Tony shouted.

Before Tom could take a breath to answer, he was knocked to the ground; the weight of a snarling corpse holding him down on the blacktop. His arms were pinned under him. He struggled to twist around and aim the pistol but couldn't turn over, the zombie was much too heavy.

Amy saw the zombie jump forward and land on her son, but she'd been overtaken by two of them, blocking her path. She couldn't reach him. She began swinging the bat wildly; panic stricken at the thought of her son being bitten, trying to hit either of them so she could reach her son but they were uncannily staying just out of her reach. It was as if they were holding her back deliberately, taunting her and waiting for their dead friend to take a bite out of Tom so they could join in.

Amy blocked out what they looked like, didn't think about the stench they gave off either as she tried to edge forward, her weight balanced on her good leg.

She thought they were both finished, knowing that even Tony wouldn't be able to get there in time to help and even though Sophie was a great shot there was no way for her to take any of the dead down without possibly hitting either her or Tom.

Suddenly a mountain bike spun to a halt next to her son. Amy couldn't see what was happening, couldn't even see who was riding it, but she heard a loud 'thump'. The next thing she knew, Tom was wrapping his arm around her and pulling her away, trying to get to the gas station and the SUV.

"Let's go Mom, just hop as fast as you can!" he said. "I don't know who that kid is but he saved our asses!"

Billy had decided he was going to pick up a game console, so he headed to the little strip mall in town where he knew there was a game store. He'd forgotten the name of the place because it was pretty generic sounding. Billy was never much of a gamer, but he thought it might be a fun way to kill time in the freight car.

He saw the guy get tackled by a zombie, with an older woman surrounded right next to him. Without even thinking he sped up and to his utter relief, got there just in time; unlike when he met Joe the previous day. The zombie hadn't yet been able to sink his teeth into the man he had pinned down.

After whacking the dead guy on the ground, Billy went after the two that were facing off against the older woman and bashed their skulls in without hesitation.

"Get her out of here," he called out to Tom. "I'll cover you!"

More dead came trudging into the street, but he was ready for them.

"Thanks for the save!" Tony said, coming up behind him. He shot one of the dead down with the .38 Tom had passed to him in the street, then stuck it in his belt and swung his own bat at another. "I would have lost my son and wife without you!"

"Not a problem." Billy replied, knocking the knees out from a zombie that was way too tall for him to hit in the head, and then bashing its skull in as it crumbled to the ground. "I'm just really glad to have been here in time."

The two were back to back, smashing down the dead as they virtually poured out of the store and the side of the building. Tony could hear the SUV approaching behind him as he saw even more of the dead lumber into the street from the nearby stores.

"Hey kid, there's too many of them." Tony put his hand on Billy's shoulder. "Let's get out of here while we still can!"

Billy didn't want to leave his bike, but the man was right. They'd taken down at least a dozen of them, but there were too many coming at them now. There was no way for them to continue without eventually being overwhelmed.

"Okay." Billy said, following Tony to

the SUV that had just pulled up right behind them.

Amy was driving. She swung the truck around to avoid the horde rapidly filling the street and floored it, grateful that her uninjured leg was the one she was using to drive.

The interior of the SUV was silent as they sped away from the scene. When they had traveled nearly a mile, Billy broke the silence.

"My name's Billy." He said quietly, hoping the people he had trusted himself with weren't nasty.

"I'm Tony, this is my wife Amy." He gestured to his wife.

"I'm Sophie, and this is Tom." She

pointed to her brother with a tired grin. "And in spite of the fact that he is my brother and a jerk sometimes, I'm really glad you helped him out back there; my Mom too."

"You guys are a family?" Billy asked shyly.

"Yeah," Amy turned and grinned at him. "We're just out on a nice drive trying to get some gas and snacks. Couldn't you tell."

Billy chuckled at her sarcasm, know how she must have felt.

"Billy, you rode up on a bike." Tony turned around in the passenger seat to look at him. "That must be a great way to travel."

"It is. It's quiet, I never run out of gas, and if I wear thick clothes," he pulled on the sleeve of his coat, "they can't hurt me even if one of them tries to bit me."

"I was going to ask you why you were dressed that way." Tony grinned, "I mean, it is a little warm for that stuff."

"That's amazing though." Amy said. "I would never have thought of that. You're a really smart kid."

Billy felt himself smile proudly. He felt it, because he wasn't used to doing it anymore, not since the dead started walking. He decided it was a nice feeling to have again.

"Are you alone?" Tony asked, hoping he wasn't asking a bad question.

Billy was reluctant to answer, not knowing the people he was with at all, but they didn't strike him as threatening.

"Yeah, I've been a lone since it all started." He replied sheepishly. "I don't mind though. It's easy for me to get around and I don't have to answer to anyone."

"How do you live?" Amy asked, sounding concerned. "Do you even have a safe place to stay?"

"Yeah, I have a really safe place." His face brightened. "I made it myself."

Billy thought for a moment, and then threw caution to the wind, trusting his instincts about the people he had helped.

"Look, normally I wouldn't do this because there are a lot of sick people out there, and I don't mean the dead people; but if you need a place to stop and rest for a while I'll show you where I'm staying. It's pretty close to where we are."

"Sounds great to me," Amy grinned. "We can all use a little rest, and I need to look at this ankle. That thing that grabbed me didn't break the skin but it hurts like hell to even stand."

FIVE

Paul Reminer watched it all come down from the roof of the hardware store across the street in silence. He turned around and looked at his two partners, Ronald Sikes and Sid Benedict, with a wide happy grin on his tanned face.

"We've been watching that kid come in and out of town now for over a week, coming and going like he owns everything. We could have had him yesterday, but now I'm glad we waited." Remy said. "His new friends are armed, but we can take them, right?"

"Remy, the only good thing I saw was the women." Sikes smirked at him wickedly. "To me they're worth more than gold around these parts."

"You better watch yourself. I remember how quick you went through the last one we had." He mocked wincing, "Not a pretty sight when you were done. I felt really bad when she killed herself."

"We should have just taken them out while they were trapped. It would have been easy, just take the last AR-15 we've got and blow them all away, walking dead included." Sid said dryly. "No fuss no muss. They might even have something we can use in that truck."

"Vicious little bastard, aren't ya?" Remy said half laughing. "But I guess we could have used their weapons, seeing how low we are on ammo ourselves."

"I just want to get things done and over with." Sid glanced at Remy, and then lit a cigarette. "We don't need anything long and drawn out."

"I know what you mean," Sikes turned to face him. "But wouldn't it be nice to have those bitches at least for a while? Maybe even that truck? We haven't had a decent ride in weeks."

"I can do you both one better." Remy's eyes brightened as he turned away from them and sat back in a lounge chair that had been on the roof when they got there a short time ago.

The three of them met during the outbreak. Sid and Remy were in the army, having gone AWOL when they realized they were fighting a losing battle. Sikes was a security guard in a bank at the time. They came together while fighting a horde of the dead outside a grocery store where the three of them were trying to get supplies. They didn't care who they shot down that day, living or dead, they just knew they needed supplies and nothing was going to stop them.

"What are you talking about?" Sid asked,

sipping from a silver flask that he kept in his pocket.

"Well, while you two were snoring away last night I went out and did some tracking." Remy exhaled a cloud of smoke and looked at them menacingly. "I know where our little young friend has been holding up, and it's a lot nicer than the roof here, in spite of our wonderful looking tents." He said sarcastically, gesturing to their camp on the roof, the cigarette in his hand leaving a trail. "I've got a plan to make it ours if you two want in. We need a permanent place to live. You can do what you want with the people, I just want the kid's hangout."

*****

"I can't believe you did all this by

yourself!" Tony said, absolutely amazed at Billy's handy work when they got inside the freight car a short time later. "This whole set-up, it's fantastic, like something you'd see in a movie."

"Dude, you've got the best horror movies too." Tom said, smacking Billy in the back after glancing over at a stack of DVDs.

"Thanks." Billy was beaming. He'd never been treated like that before, as if he were really smart or cool; as if he were someone. "The air mattress is further down, just turn on the lamps along the way so you can see better. You can take your Mom down there if you want. There are pillows and blankets too. I wish I had an ace bandage, but my first-aid kit is a bit limited." He said to Tom, who was helping his Mom along.

"We'll figure something out," Amy said. "We're just grateful, I'm grateful, that you brought us here. After what we've been going through it's like heaven."

"It's okay, really." Billy smiled at her as Tom brought her to the back of the car.

Before he could turn back around to speak to Tony, he felt himself get spun around and hugged tightly. It was Sophie. She pulled away and gave him a kiss on the cheek.

"That was for saving us," she grinned, then kissed him again on the other cheek, "and that was just for the hell of it." She laughed, even harder when she saw how red Billy got when he blushed.

Sophie didn't seem much older than he was, but he was not used to getting that sort of attention, in fact, unless he was getting picked on in school, and sometimes even at home, he wasn't used to getting any attention at all.

Tony motioned over to him.

"So nobody can get in here?" He asked, trying not to laugh at how Billy was still red in the face.

"Not unless they can get up the ladder and in through that opening. I mean, I have an escape hatch in case I ever had to get out fast, too. It's in the floor over by the bathroom." He replied, relieved to feel his face finally cool off. "The side doors are locked up tight on both sides."

"You've got a bathroom here?" Tony said, brow raised skeptically.

"Well, it's a portable RV toilet. It runs on a hand pump but it does use water. It doesn't smell too bad." He confirmed. "I found a store that carried camping equipment. That's where I got a lot of this stuff. It just took me a few trips and a little while to get things set up. I don't like stealing but I didn't have any choice."

"You're a genius. I wouldn't be too worried about the stealing part though, the world is a different place now. Hell, I'm completely blown away by all this." Tony said, looking around. "Do you think the truck is safe where I parked it, or should I try to hide it somehow?"

"I'll be honest with you, not many of the dead come around here. I see a few here and there, but usually the cameras are clear each time I check."

"If you say so, and you would know." Tony nodded, sounding relieved. He stepped away to check on his wife.

Billy got together a few cans of spaghetti and heated them up on the propane stove. He was happy but felt disoriented, as if having Tony and his family there had somehow put off his normal routine. In a sense it did, but he seriously thought that it was a good thing and not a bad thing. It was just something he had to get used to.

His world had changed yet again.

When the spaghetti was hot he dished it

out to all of them with some bottled water, cold from the battery powered cooler he had.

They sat in the back of the car so they could be near Amy, who was lying down with her ankle wrapped and her foot propped up.

"Mom's ankle doesn't look too bad. I hope you don't mind, I tore one of your shirts into strips to use as a bandage." Tom said. "I thought wrapping it for support would help."

"Don't even worry about it. I've got clothes piled up all over the place." He nodded.

"I never thought canned spaghetti would taste so good." Tony said, digging in. "I can understand how you kept the water cold because I saw the cooler, but how'd you heat this up?"

"Yeah, do you have a microwave down here or something?" Sophie asked. "Not that I'd be surprised if you did."

"No, I didn't want to bring a microwave in because most of them use too much power. It would drain my batteries too much too quickly." He nodded at them. "I've got a propane stove. It's got two burners and runs off of those small propane cylinders. I've got a couple of cases of them so I don't have to keep hunting them down. They seemed in short supply wherever I went."

"I've never used one of those before. Do you think it's dangerous being enclosed like this?" Tony asked.

"I don't think so. I've never had any trouble with it," he said thoughtfully, "then again I don't use it very often, and when I do it's for no more than a few minutes at a time. I don't think it would be a good idea to smoke around it because I'm paranoid of the propane, but I don't smoke so it never mattered."

Tony nodded at him.

"If you guys want to get some rest there's a pile of blankets by the wall." Billy pointed across the car. "I want to go check the batteries and the cameras. It's sort of my evening routine."

"A little rest would do us all some good." Tony said.

"Hey Tony, do you think you can give me a ride back to get my bike tomorrow?" Billy asked timidly. "Those dead people should be gone by then."

"Hey that's the least I can do." He smiled, "Thanks again, for everything you've done. I don't think any of us would have survived today without you."

Amy watched Billy walk away. She shook her head, looking confused.

"I don't understand how he could have done all this." She said to Tony quietly. "I mean, he can't be more than a year or two younger than Sophie. I feel so bad for him, he's so alone."

"He's really smart, but I think even more so he's damn brave to be out here like this alone. Look around though, he's got all the comforts of home. It's a like the ultimate 'Man-Cave' but secure enough to keep the dead riffraff out." He pointed to where the toilet was. "He's even got an escape hatch by the toilet. It's in the floor."

"He's thought of everything." Amy laid back. "Maybe we should see about having him help us set another freight car up. Besides, I think Sophie likes him." She chuckled.

"Yeah, I think so too, and staying here is actually not a bad idea." He smirked, looking at his son and daughter lying down next to the air mattress. They had already dosed off. "Maybe we should talk to him tomorrow."

SIX

Sid and Sikes both decided Remy's plan was worthwhile, and feasible, so they packed all their ammo, the AR-15, and the two Berettas that were in working order. They had a shotgun, but only four shells for it, so they considered it dead weight and left it at their camp on the roof.

It took them hours to travel safely

through town after dark even though it was a clear night. The stars were bright enough to light up the streets, but the trio still had many obstacles to avoid. They knew all the areas where the dead were in high numbers from their roof surveillance, and had to trek around all of them until they could finally reach the train station.

Crouched down between two abandoned cars, they waited for a pack of zombies to pass through the parking lot at the front of the building. Remy told them that he'd seen the same group circle it several times the last time he was there.

"It's like they have their own territory or some kind of crazy routine or something." Remy whispered. "We've gotta move as soon as they pass us and get to that side street." He pointed to the road that ran parallel to the train tracks.

"How do we get the ones we need to use?" Sikes said, annoyed at how difficult their trip had been. "It's not like we can invite a couple without having to deal with the rest of them."

"Don't worry about that. There are always a few lurking around one of the houses a couple blocks away. We can coax them out when we need to, but you have to be quiet or it'll bring more of them into the mix and we'll be fucked big-time."

They made a run for it, narrowly avoiding the dead that just prowled past them.

The strongest of the three, Sid was carrying the AR-15. He stayed behind Remy and Sikes. They didn't have as much ammo as he would have preferred, but he thought it was more than enough for what they needed to do.

"If everything goes well, we might not even need to use it." He thought to himself.

They'd had a difficult time getting ammo and more guns of late. Anything that had been left on the streets had been ruined by the elements. The ammo was still good, but ammo without a gun for it was useless. Most of the gun shops they found had been cleaned out of just about everything too.

Sid knew Remy was right when it came to how they were living. They needed a safe place where they could stay long-term without the need to be constantly searching for weapons or a place to sleep.

"I just wish they'd have let me kill them when I wanted to so we wouldn't have to be going through all this crazy shit right now." He thought angrily.

They traveled for about a quarter of a mile before Remy pointed out the zombies they were going to use.

"It's all yours Sikes. Make it look like you're really unarmed and terrified of them. Run and yell a lot. Maybe you can even limp a little." Remy said urgently. "The sooner they hear you, the sooner you draw them out. We need at least a couple of them outside before we make our move."

"Where the fuck are you gonna be while I'm putting my ass on the line being bait for those dead bastards?" Sikes asked, slipping his Beretta in the back waistband of his pants.

"Like I told you before, we'll be following along the tree-line, just out of sight. We've got your back, don't worry about it." Remy assured him.

Sikes nodded, and made his move.

*****

Billy dosed off for a while on the couch, but then woke up and couldn't get back to sleep again. He was tired but felt energized somehow, wide awake. He decided to check the cameras and see what the night looked like before trying to go back to sleep again.

While he stared at the individual feeds, he couldn't help but think about how the events of the previous day had changed his life.

So much had changed already that he nearly didn't recognize himself. He had so many ideals growing up that he'd hope to maintain all his life. He never counted on the outbreak, and how he'd have to cross so many lines in his life. But now there was a whole family staying with him; even a girl that he thought was cute.

"She doesn't make fun of me either," he mumbled, feeling his face warm at the memory of her hug.

A shadow moving down the street, near the SUV abruptly caught his eye on one of the camera feeds and he immediately sat up to take a closer look, trying to zoom in.

"What the hell?" He muttered under his breath when he saw a man being chased by a couple of zombies.

The man started to shout. He was so loud Billy could even hear him inside the freight car without the microphones on the cameras.

"What's going on?" Tony said, rubbing his eyes. He and his son had run up from the back of the freight car and Billy could hear Sophie and Amy calling out too.

"There's somebody out there, and it looks like he's being chased." Billy shook his head and pointed to the screen. "I think he may be hurt, it looks like he's limping." He made the picture larger so they could all see it more clearly. "I don't think he's armed, but so far he's holding his own just by staying out of their reach. If he keeps yelling like that though he's going to attract more of them."

"We better get out there and help him." Tony looked at his son. "Get the shotgun and a bat."

Tom ran off to the back where they had their stuff and Sophie came up a few seconds later.

"What are you gonna do?" She asked her father nervously.

"Just stay here with your Mom." Tony said. He looked at Billy. "We're gonna go out and try to help him. Can you stay here with the girls just in case something goes wrong?"

Billy didn't know what to say, but he thought it was really strange, someone nearby being chased by zombies when normally there weren't any around at all. Then again he never expected to find Tony and his family in the strip mall either.

"Alright, but I'll keep an eye out." He said, uneasy. "I don't like the looks of this at all."

"Sophie, you better take this in case we run into trouble." Tom said when he returned with the bat and the shotgun. He handed her the .38 from his belt.

"We've got your back." She said, looking at Billy. "Right?"

Billy nodded.

Tony and Tom climbed the ladder and

got on the roof. Crouched over, they checked around to see if there were any more of the dead besides the ones chasing the guy below. When they didn't see any, they climbed the ladder down and ran toward the man, who was much closer to the freight car now then he was when they saw him on camera.

"I'll get them," Tony said, brandishing the bat. "Don't shoot unless you see me in trouble."

"I'd say you're both in trouble." Remy said, exhaling a cloud of smoke as he stepped out of the shadows. He pointed his revolver at Tony. "Now just put the bat down, and tell your son to drop the rifle nice and slow."

Tony's face became a mask of anger. He dropped the bat and waved for Tom to put the shotgun down.

"I'm sorry Tom, but it looks like we've been tricked by this worthless piece of shit!" Tony growled furiously.

"Such a bleeding heart, I bet you were a liberal before the world went to shit." Sid said, smacking Tony in the head with the butt of the AR-15. Tony went down hard as Sid retrieved the bat and the shotgun. He retreated several yards but turned the AR-15 at Tom. "Don't get any ideas about being a hero kid, it'll only get you and everyone else killed."

"I don't know how long I can hold these things off without shooting them." Sikes shouted.

"Just hang on for a bit longer." Remy said, stepping on his cigarette. "I'm going in the freight car. They won't give me any trouble with these guys at gunpoint."

*****

Billy saw that they had been tricked and cursed himself for letting it happen.

"Damn it! I should have known it was a trick!" He slammed a fist on the tabletop.

"What are we gonna do?" Sophie said. "I've still got the .38. Do you have any guns here?"

"I've never fired a gun in my life. Out of all the things I promised myself I'd never do, that's the one thing I'm sticking with." His mind raced and he quickly came up with a plan. He looked over at where he had the propane stove and grinned.

"Sophie, go get your Mom and get out of here. There's a door in the floor by the toilet. It's only held in with deadbolts so all you have to do is slide them open. I don't think they'll be able to see you getting out. Maybe you can get the jump on the others with your gun. That guy's gonna be here any minute, so you've got to hurry."

"Well, what are you gonna do?" Sophie said, confused.

"I've got a plan that will help you guys get away to safety. You're a family, the only one I've seen since all this started. It's important that you stay together and stay alive." Billy said sternly. "Now get out of here before it's too late!"

"Okay, but I owe you one, we all do." Sophie kissed him lightly on the lips and smiled, then turned away and raced toward her mother. "Consider that partial payment." She called out along the way.

Billy felt warm inside. He'd never had a girl kiss him like that before. Sadly he couldn't let the feeling linger; he knew he didn't have time. The sound of footsteps on the roof told him he had a minute or two at most to do what he knew he had to do.

"No matter what any of them say, they'll never let us live, at least not Tony, Tom and I. I don't even want to think about what they'll do to Sophie and her Mom." He thought angrily.

The boxes of propane were behind the table near the far wall. He ran over to them and quickly started opening the valves on as many as he could. He got through nearly a dozen, and could smell the propane filling the air in that corner of the freight car. When he heard the door in the ceiling flip open he raced to the propane stove itself and turned it on without hitting the igniter. He could hear the hiss of the propane and smiled.

"We're willing to let you all live, you just have to get out of here. All of you. This place is ours now." Remy called out, climbing down inside the freight car, holding out his gun. He expected to see the two women and the kid waiting for him. All he saw was the kid, and he was smiling like he just heard the funniest joke.

"Hi. My names Billy," he said, still grinning.

"I don't care what you call yourself." Remy snarled, "Where's the rest of them? We have the men outside, there's still two women. Where'd they go?"

"One of them is injured. It's her ankle. She was resting in the back, so the other one went to help her come up here." Billy said. "Hey, you don't by any chance have an extra cigarette, do you?"

"Sure kid." He tossed him an open pack with matches stuck in the wrapper. "If you're lying about the women it'll be the last one you ever smoke."

"I don't smoke," he slipped the matches

out of the package. "And besides never using a gun, that's a line I'll never cross. I'm quite sure of that."

He lit a match and the freight car filled with flames, then exploded.

EPILOGUE

Sophie succeeded in getting her mother out of the freight car. It was a struggle but together they made it up to the front of the flat car, ahead of the freight car and safely away from everyone else. Seconds later, when the freight car went up, the force of the explosion knocked everyone to the ground.

Sophie had no idea what happened, but

being the furthest away, she was also the first able to get to her feet. After checking on her mother, she looked around.

The freight car had been blown open on the far side and was in flames. She didn't see Billy anywhere, but forced herself to ignore her concern while she, still shaken from the blast, staggered around the burning car and down to the street.

"Oh no, you don't!" She shouted, seeing Sid try to rise. She pulled the .38 out and shot him twice in the center of his chest before he could stand and raise the AR-15 again.

Sikes, on the ground next to the fallen zombies, turned over and watched Sophie shoot Sid. Rather than pull his own gun out he forced himself to stand and run.

It was over, they lost and he knew it.

The explosion and fire brought more zombies to the area. Tony, a deep gash in his head gathered his family together and made a run for the SUV. Surprisingly it was undamaged by the freight car's fiery demise.

"Somehow he must have used the propane to save us." Tony shook his head, wishing he could have done something to stop him.

"He didn't have to do that!" Sophie cried, "We could have figured something out, a different way!"

"I'm sorry honey," Amy said, crying herself. "He did what he thought was best. He was a very brave young man."

The dead came toward them, dozens of them. Amy started the truck and said a silent prayer for Billy. She put it in gear and floored it down the street, away from what was once Billy's sanctuary.

"All I can say is, thanks, Billy." Tony said sadly, taking one last look at the flaming freight car.

ABOUT THE AUTHOR

Nick Kisella grew up in Manville, New Jersey where he began writing fantasy and horror while still in high school. Some of his first published work appeared in Indie magazines during the '80s. Since then his work has appeared in various forms from print and online magazines to blogs. His first fantasy novel, 'The Emerald and the Blade' came out in 1989 by a long defunct publisher, with 'The Chalice of Souls' soon to follow. Some of his more recent work includes a screenplay and novelization for 'Nifty Entertainment' a California based Indie production company, as well as getting the first two fantasy novels he wrote as a teen, 'The Chalice of Souls' and 'Death and the Doomweaver' back in print for the sheer nostalgia of it. 'Morningstars', his first full-length horror novel was published by Black Bed Sheet Books in 2012. 'The Beasts and the Walking Dead' a post-apocalyptic fiction novel, also published by Black Bed Sheet

Books is the first part of a series. He wrote the novelization to the James Balsamo film, 'I Spill Your Guts', and recently finished novelizations for Ryan Scott Weber's films, 'Mary Horror', 'Sheriff Tom versus the Zombies' and 'Witches Blood'. 'Crossing Lines' is the second prequel to 'The Beasts and the Walking Dead', preceded by the recent novel 'Under Construction'.

Always having an eventful life, he writes when time allows, usually after dark.

A fitness enthusiast, he has been a certified fitness instructor involved in the industry for twenty years, and continues to stay in shape and train individuals while in his late 40s.

Nick resides in Northeastern Pennsylvania with his Kimberly and their twins.

For news relating to new releases, appearances, or to purchase signed books visit:
WWW.NickKisella.com

To contact Nick Kisella look for him on Facebook :
https://www.facebook.com/nick.kisella

Crossing Lines
A Weber Pictures Publication
Cover Art By Ryan Scott Weber
Nick Kisella's photo by Stan Stronski

Made in the USA
Charleston, SC
10 October 2014